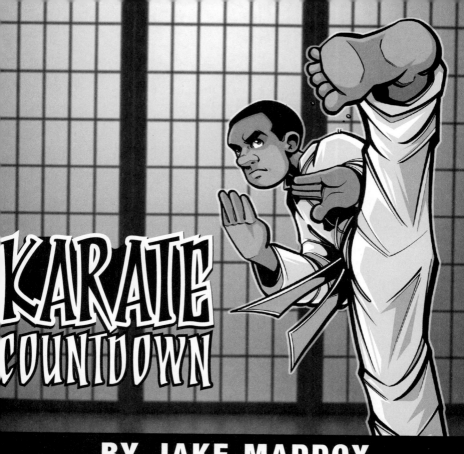

KARATE COUNTDOWN

BY JAKE MADDOX

illustrated by Sean Tiffany

text by Eric Stevens

Impact Books are published by Stone Arch Books
151 Good Counsel Drive, P.O. Box 669
Mankato, Minnesota 56002
www.stonearchbooks.com

Library of Congress Cataloging-in-Publication Data
Maddox, Jake.
    Karate Countdown / by Jake Maddox; illustrated by Sean Tiffany.
    p. cm. — (Impact Books. A Jake Maddox Sports Story)
    ISBN 978-1-4342-1200-9 (library binding)
    ISBN 978-1-4342-1402-7 (pbk.)
    [1. Karate—Fiction. 2. Anger—Fiction.] I. Tiffany, Sean, ill.
II. Title.
PZ7.M25643Kan 2009
[Fic]—dc22   2008031958

Summary:
When Kenny's anger problem gets out of control, his father signs him
up for karate lessons. But even in karate class, Kenny can't get a grip on
his temper. He's getting a reputation for being angry. With help from
his karate teacher, will Kenny be able to calm down long enough to
focus—and win?

Creative Director: Heather Kindseth
Graphic Designer: Carla Zetina-Yglesias

1 2 3 4 5 6 14 13 12 11 10 09

Printed in the United States of America

TABLE OF CONTENTS

CHAPTER 1

TROUBLE

Kenny Parks leaned against the passenger window of his dad's car. They were driving down Elm Street after a meeting with the principal at Kenny's school. The school year had just started, and Kenny was already in trouble.

"I'm pretty disappointed with you, Ken," his dad said. "I really thought that this year was going to be different from last year."

Ever since his mother died, Kenny seemed to get in trouble all the time. For some reason, Kenny would get angry very easily. He would talk back to teachers. Sometimes he even yelled at them.

"I just wish I knew why you can't get along with any of your teachers," his dad said as he turned onto their street.

Kenny shrugged. "It's not my fault, Dad," he said. "Teachers never like me!"

Kenny dropped his head. His mom had been a teacher, but that was a long time ago. "Look, Dad, I'm sorry," Kenny said.

Dad parked the car in front of their house. "I know you're sorry, Ken," he said. "You're always sorry, but nothing has changed. I think it's time to do something about this."

Kenny felt his face get hot. "What do you mean?" he asked.

"Well, when I was a boy, I used to get angry sometimes," Dad said. "So I took a karate class. It really helped."

Dad had often talked about his childhood karate lessons. He had really loved them, and he wanted Kenny to love karate too. But besides shooting hoops with his friends, Kenny had never been a big fan of sports. He wasn't interested in lessons of any kind.

Kenny rolled his eyes. "I don't want to take karate lessons, Dad," he said. He opened his car door.

Dad put his hand on Kenny's arm. "Sorry, Ken," Dad said. "It's already done. I signed you up for a class. Your first lesson is this Saturday at eight."

"Eight in the morning?" Kenny replied, nearly shouting. "On a Saturday? That's not fair!"

Dad got out of the car and walked toward their house. His keys jingled in his hands.

"Maybe it's not fair," Dad said. "But we've got to do something about how you've been acting."

Kenny followed him across the yard toward the front door of their house. "Dad!" he said.

"It's final, Ken," Dad replied. "You're learning karate." He opened the front door and walked inside.

Great, Kenny thought. *So much for my weekends.*

CHAPTER 2

ROBES

Most weeks, Kenny looked forward to the weekend. Usually, it felt like the weekend would never come. But that week, Kenny was not excited about the weekend. For some reason, the week flew by. Before Kenny knew it, his alarm clock was going off. It was 7:30 a.m. on Saturday.

"Rise and shine, Ken!" his dad called from the kitchen. "I'm making sausage and biscuits for breakfast."

Kenny took a deep breath through his nose. He could smell the sausage and gravy, and the biscuits in the oven.

Well, Kenny thought, *at least I'll get an awesome breakfast.*

"We need to leave in 15 minutes," Dad said. "You can't be late for your first day of karate class!"

"Okay," Kenny called. "I'm coming."

Kenny threw on some jeans and a T-shirt. He sat down at the kitchen table and started wolfing down his breakfast.

"What are you wearing?" his dad asked, smirking.

Kenny stopped eating. He looked down at his T-shirt and jeans. "What?" he said. "I always dress like this."

Dad shook his head. "Not this morning," he said. "Take a look in the gym bag on the chair next to you."

Kenny frowned. He reached over and grabbed the bag.

"What is it?" he asked.

"Open it," Dad replied.

Kenny opened the bag. He looked inside and pulled out a heavy white shirt and a pair of white pants.

"Karate robes!" his dad said, smiling.

"Are you kidding me?" Kenny asked, eyes wide. "I have to wear this thing?"

Dad got up to refill his coffee. "Of course," he said. "What did you think you would wear for karate?"

"I'll look like an idiot!" Kenny said.

Dad sipped his coffee and sat down with the paper. "Nah," he said, "you'll look like everyone else in your class. Go get dressed."

"Come on!" Kenny yelled. "This is so dumb!"

Without looking up from his newspaper, Kenny's dad said, "Try saying thank you instead. These karate lessons and robes aren't free, you know."

Kenny started to walk back to his room. But his dad stood up. "Wait a second, Kenny," Dad said. "Don't forget your belt!"

Dad reached out and handed Kenny a white strip of cloth. "At first, you'll wear a white belt with your robes," Dad explained. "As you get better and better, you'll get a new belt as you reach each new level. It's pretty cool."

Kenny rolled his eyes as he grabbed the belt from his dad. He stomped back down the hall to his room to change.

Could this day get any worse? he thought.

CHAPTER 3

SENSEI

The karate school was in a little mall. It was near the bus station.

"This is it?" Kenny asked as his dad parked out front. "This place looks gross."

"Don't judge a book by its cover," Dad replied. "I'll pick you up in an hour."

Kenny sighed as he climbed out of the car. He slammed the car door behind him and headed for the karate school.

"Welcome," a small man said as Kenny walked in. "Please stand along the wall with the other students."

"Okay," Kenny replied. He looked to his right. About ten other guys were already there, dressed in robes and white belts just like him. They were standing against the wall, staring straight ahead.

The small man wore a black belt with his white robes. Kenny had heard enough about karate from his dad to know that a black belt meant the man was a karate master.

Kenny walked over to an empty spot near the middle of the group. "What is this, the army?" he joked to the kid next to him.

The kid smiled, but didn't look at him or reply. Kenny shrugged.

"Students," said the small man at the front of the room, "thank you for joining our karate class."

The man bowed. Kenny watched as the other students bowed back at him. Quickly, he followed their lead and bowed as well.

"We will begin today with how to tie your belt," the teacher said. "I can see that some of your belts are a little sloppy. Please remove them and I will show you the correct way to tie them."

The other students all undid their belts. Kenny chuckled. "Next he's going to show us how to tie our shoes!" he said to the guy next to him.

"If your shoes are as sloppy as your belt," the teacher said, "then, yes, I will help you with your shoes."

Kenny rolled his eyes. "My robe is closed," Kenny replied. "I guess my belt is doing its job."

"The belt does not only close the robe," the teacher answered. "It shows others what kind of student you are."

"Then I guess I'm a sloppy student, sir," Kenny said. His voice was tense and angry.

"Sensei," the teacher replied sternly. "In karate, we use the Japanese word *sensei*, not *sir*."

Kenny felt his face getting hot. He yanked off his belt.

"And we reply, 'Yes, Sensei,'" the man added.

Kenny looked down at the floor. "Yes, Sensei," he said quietly.

CHAPTER 4

MONDAY

Monday morning was almost a relief to Kenny. He had been sore from his karate class for the entire weekend. After learning how to tie their belts, the class had done a bunch of jumping jacks and sit-ups to warm up. Then Sensei had showed them how to punch.

Kenny slouched in his chair before his first class at school on Monday morning. He rubbed his shoulder.

"What's wrong with you?" Craig Peters asked from the desk next to Kenny.

"My whole body is sore," Kenny replied.

"Did you get in a fight again this weekend?" Craig asked.

"No, I didn't get in a fight," Kenny snapped. "Why, do you want to start something?"

Craig laughed and threw up his hands. "Easy, buddy," he said.

Craig had known Kenny for years, and he knew Kenny wouldn't start a real fight with him. They were friends. But he had seen Kenny in a few bad fights over the years with other kids.

Kenny scowled. "My dad signed me up for karate lessons," he said.

"Nice!" Craig replied. He sliced the air with one hand, then the other. "Hiya!" he said.

Kenny rolled his eyes.

"You'll be a ninja in no time," Craig added.

"It's not like that at all, believe me," Kenny said.

"It's not?" Craig asked. "No wicked chops and flying kicks and fighting ten ninjas at once?"

Kenny just shook his head. "Not at all," he said. "It's more like making the students feel like idiots and showing them how to tie their shoes."

The bell rang. "Okay, class," Ms. Riaz announced. "Let's get started."

"Tie their shoes?" Craig whispered, leaning over.

Kenny nodded. "Pretty much," he said. "It's really stupid."

CHAPTER 5

CONTROL

That week went by fast. It wasn't a terrible week. There were no meetings with the principal, but Kenny did talk back a few times to Ms. Riaz.

At karate class on Saturday, Kenny lined up with the other students. He made sure his belt was tied correctly.

Sensei bowed. Kenny bowed back with the other students.

"Today," Sensei said, "we will work on blocking. You will be able to defend yourselves against the punches we learned last week."

Sensei stepped to the center of the mat. "I will show you several blocks before we begin," he said. "Mr. Parks, you will attack."

Kenny opened his eyes wide. "Me?" he asked, shocked.

"Me, Sensei," the teacher corrected. "And yes, you, Mr. Parks. Please stand here in your punching stance."

Kenny stepped forward and stood on the mat. He faced Sensei. Then he spread his feet and bent his elbows. He was in the punching stance he had learned the week before.

"Good stance, Mr. Parks," the teacher said. "Attack me whenever you feel like you are ready."

"You want me to punch you, Sensei?" Kenny asked, surprised.

"I want you to try to punch me," Sensei replied, smiling.

Kenny inhaled deeply and clenched his fists. He thought back to the last week of class and remembered the way to do a punch to the chest.

He took a step forward. With a loud grunt, he punched.

As fast as lightning, Sensei blocked the punch with his left arm. Then, before Kenny could pull his arm back, Sensei lifted him by the elbow and dropped him onto his back.

In less than a second, Sensei was standing over Kenny. Kenny stared up at him from the mat.

"Ow," Kenny moaned.

Sensei turned to the class. "Do you see, students," he said, "how I used Mr. Parks's energy against him?"

"Yes, Sensei!" the others replied.

Kenny was angry. Sensei had made him look like a fool!

Kenny jumped to his feet and ran at his teacher. "Block this!" he yelled. He charged at the small man.

"Gladly," Sensei replied. He calmly stepped aside and gently caught Kenny by the shoulder. In less than a second, Kenny was on his back again.

Sensei kneeled over Kenny. "Mr. Parks," the teacher said quietly. "You must learn to control your anger. Otherwise, your anger will control you." He reached out his hand to help Kenny up.

Kenny got to his feet with Sensei's help. "That's easy for you to say," Kenny said under his breath.

* * *

An hour later, class was over. Sensei had been Kenny's partner for all the sparring. Somehow, Kenny had managed to stay on his feet most of the time, except whenever he'd gotten angry.

The class lined up. "Very well done today, students," Sensei said. "I will let you go in a moment. First, I have an announcement."

Kenny glanced at the other students. All of them kept their eyes straight ahead.

"In three weeks," Sensei continued, "we will have a class tournament. Every year, we hold a tournament for the students in each level's class."

He smiled. "Being in the tournament is required," Sensei added. "The winner of the tournament will earn the respect of his Sensei and his classmates. He will also receive free lessons for the next level of training."

Some of the students smiled or cheered. "Cool," said the guy next to Kenny.

"Thank you, students," Sensei finished. He bowed. All of the students, including Kenny, bowed back. Then they headed outside to wait for their rides home.

"Man, I really want to win that tournament," a kid said to Kenny as they waited.

Kenny shrugged. "I doubt I have a chance," he said. "Did you see the way Sensei threw me around in there?"

The other kid laughed. "That just means you get more practice than the rest of us," he said. "And sparring against Sensei is better practice than sparring against one of us."

Kenny nodded. "That's true," he replied.

The other kid kept talking, but Kenny wasn't paying attention to him.

Hmm, Kenny thought. *Maybe I do have a shot at winning the tournament.*

CHAPTER 6

MELTDOWN

"Another rough karate lesson?" Craig asked before class on Monday.

Kenny groaned. "You know it," he replied.

"What happened?" his friend asked. "Did the teacher pick on you again?"

Kenny nodded. "Even worse than last time," he replied. He rolled up the sleeve of his T-shirt. There was a big purple bruise.

"Whoa!" Craig said. "That's a nice one. How'd you get that?"

Kenny shook his head. "Man, you wouldn't believe me," he said.

"Try me," Craig said.

Kenny looked around the classroom before answering to make sure no one was listening. "I attacked him on Saturday," he whispered.

"The teacher? You attacked your teacher?" Craig asked, stunned.

Kenny nodded slowly, smiling a little. "Can you believe it?" he asked.

"To be honest, yes!" Craig replied. "I think you'd attack Jackie Chan if he made you angry."

Ms. Riaz walked in. Then the bell rang.

"Don't start with me, Craig!" Kenny said quietly. Craig chuckled and opened his notebook.

"Good morning, everyone," Ms. Riaz said. "Can I have three volunteers write the answers for the homework on the board, please?"

Kenny looked around. As usual, no one volunteered.

After a moment, Ms. Riaz sighed. "Okay then, I'll choose three people," she said.

Everyone, including Kenny, slouched a little in their seats. No one wanted to be chosen.

"Okay, question number one, Hanna," Ms. Riaz said. Hanna stood up.

"Number two, Jay, please," Ms. Riaz went on.

"Yes," Craig said in a whisper.

"One more," Kenny said, crossing his fingers.

Ms. Riaz looked at him. She said "Kenny, come on up and do number three, please."

Craig pointed at Kenny. "You're the man," Craig said, laughing.

Kenny pulled his homework out of his notebook. He walked up to the white board.

Ms. Riaz handed him a marker. "Thank you, Kenny," she said.

Kenny glanced at the work the other two students were doing. They were going through their math problems quickly.

He looked down at his homework. His handwriting was sloppy, and he was sure his answer for question number three was wrong.

Slowly, he raised the marker. He started copying the problem onto the board.

Math, Kenny thought. *What a waste of time! Like I'll ever need to know this stuff in real life.*

He finished writing his answer on the board. Then he stood back and looked it over. He had no idea if his answer was right.

With a shrug, Kenny tossed the marker on the tray. Then he went back to his desk.

"I don't think your answer's right, man," Craig whispered as Kenny sat down. "I got 42."

Kenny looked up at his answer. He had written 117. If Craig was right, Kenny wasn't even close.

Great, Kenny thought.

He barely paid attention as the class went over the first two problems. Then it was time for number three.

"Okay, Kenny," Ms. Riaz said. "For question three, you came up with 117."

Kenny shrugged. "I guess," he said.

"Can you explain how you came up with that answer?" Ms. Riaz asked.

"No," Kenny mumbled.

"You can't explain?" Ms. Riaz asked, frowning.

"What's the point?" Kenny snapped. He knocked his textbook off his desk. It hit the ground with a thud. "I got it wrong, right?"

Ms. Riaz sighed. "Okay, Kenny," she said. "I'll talk to you after class."

* * *

When the bell rang to end the class, everyone hurried to leave. Craig whispered, "Good luck, Jackie Chan," before he left the classroom.

Ms. Riaz walked over to Kenny's desk. She said, "Kenny, this isn't the first time we've had this conversation, is it?"

Kenny shrugged. "I guess not," he said.

"I can see that these math problems are frustrating you," Ms. Riaz went on. "However, if you let your frustration take over, you'll never find the right answer."

"I know," Kenny said. He thought about all the time he spent on the mat when he sparred with Sensei.

"Do I need to set up another meeting with the principal and your father?" Ms. Riaz asked.

Kenny sighed. "No," he said. "You don't need to call my dad."

"You know, sometimes I get frustrated with a math problem," Ms. Riaz began.

"You get frustrated with math problems?" Kenny asked, shocked.

"Of course!" Ms. Riaz said. "Everyone does sometimes."

Kenny sat back in his chair. "Huh," he muttered. He wondered if Sensei ever got angry.

CHAPTER 7

BENCHED

"Today, students, we will begin with sparring," Sensei said. The students were lined up against the wall to start class.

"Mr. Parks," Sensei added, "I will let you practice with someone else today. Everyone, please choose a partner."

Everyone picked a partner. Kenny ended up with a kid named Steve Shaw. A couple of students spread their feet and got ready to do some punches.

"Students!" Sensei interrupted. "Don't forget to bow."

All the students brought their feet together. They stood up straight.

First, everyone turned to bow at Sensei. Then they turned and bowed at their partners.

"Thank you," Sensei said, smiling. "Begin!"

At first, it was pretty sloppy. Kenny got into position and pulled back a fist to punch. At the same time, Steve started to punch.

"This isn't working," Kenny said, laughing. "I'll block first."

Steve nodded. "Cool," he said. "You had all that practice punching Sensei last week anyway!"

Steve drew his elbow in and tightened his fists. Kenny was ready to block.

Steve counted off with a sharp yell. Then he moved forward and started to attack Kenny.

Kenny blocked quickly. He stopped several punches by snapping his arm across his stomach.

"Hiya!" he cried as he brushed Steve's punches aside. "Hiya!"

"Very good, Mr. Parks!" Sensei called out as he walked past them. "Try to stay focused, Mr. Shaw!" he added to Kenny's partner.

Then Kenny accidentally blocked to the right when he should have blocked to the left. One of Steve's punches got through and struck him hard in the chest.

Before he knew what had happened, Kenny was on the mat. For a moment, he felt like he couldn't breathe.

Steve leaned over him. "Are you okay?" he asked. He put out his hand to help Kenny up.

Kenny didn't take it. Instead, he slapped Steve's hand away.

"I'm fine!" Kenny snapped.

"Are you?" Sensei asked, walking over. He stood next to Steve. "You sound angry," Sensei went on. "You're letting your feelings control you."

"So what?" Kenny said. He got to his feet. Then he turned to face Steve. "It's my turn to attack," Kenny said.

"No," Sensei said. "It's your turn to sit down."

"What?" Kenny said. "That's not fair!"

"Fair?" Sensei said. "Who said anything about fair? You will sit on the bench and look at the street through the window."

Kenny clenched his fists. He felt his face getting hot.

"A bus stops in front of this school every ten minutes," Sensei added. "You will watch the bus stop and count how many people get off."

"Are you kidding me?" Kenny asked.

Sensei turned away. "Class, continue sparring, please!" he said. "The first round of the tournament is coming soon!"

Kenny was mad. He sat down on the bench and faced the window. Soon, the bus pulled up.

Well, this is boring, Kenny thought. He watched the people get off. First was an old lady. She took forever to walk down the steps.

"One," Kenny muttered.

Three high school girls stepped off after the old lady. "Two, three, and four," Kenny said.

Then the bus doors closed. It drove off.

"Four, Sensei!" Kenny called out. He turned to face the classroom again.

"Face the window, Mr. Parks," Sensei replied. "Don't call out the numbers. You will tell me later."

Kenny rolled his eyes and turned back to the window. There wasn't much to look at outside. It was just a boring street in his boring city.

Across the street was a car dealership. Next to that was a restaurant, and next to that was a grocery store. None of them were even open yet this early on a Saturday.

Kenny could hear the other students sparring behind him. "Hiya!" they cried out as they sparred.

Kenny started to get angry. He hated listening to them spar while he just sat there. Just then, the bus pulled up again. The door hissed when it opened.

A big man stepped carefully off the bus. He was carrying a paper bag. "One," Kenny muttered to himself.

A young mother followed. She was pulling her daughter behind her. The little girl was crying.

"Two, three," Kenny said. He took a deep breath.

After the mother and child, two kids about Kenny's age hopped off the bus. They were laughing and horsing around.

"Four and five," Kenny said. He took another deep breath.

Finally, a middle-aged woman stepped out, talking on her cell phone. Then the doors closed.

"Six," Kenny said. "Plus the four from before . . . that makes ten."

The morning went on like that. Kenny watched the bus stop and counted the people getting off.

By the time class was over, he didn't even notice the students behind him, even with all the yelling.

After dismissing the rest of the class, Sensei went over to Kenny. "So, Mr. Parks," Sensei said. "What did you learn today?"

"Well," Kenny said, "I counted forty-two people total."

Sensei smiled. "The number does not matter," he said.

"It doesn't?" Kenny asked. "Then why did I have to count everyone?"

"It's not the answer you needed," Sensei replied. "It's the counting itself."

"I don't get it," Kenny said.

"Did you feel calmer as you counted?" Sensei asked.

"Yes," Kenny admitted.

"Then that's what you needed," Sensei said.

CHAPTER 8

COUNTING

"Did you quit karate or something?" Craig asked the next Monday in math class. "You don't look hurt today."

"The last class was weird," Kenny said. But just then, Ms. Riaz walked in and the bell rang.

"Good morning, everyone," Ms. Riaz said. "Let's take a look at the homework. Any volunteers to show your work on the white board?"

Kenny looked around the room. As usual, no one volunteered.

"She's going to call on me, man," Kenny whispered to Craig. "I know it."

"After what happened last week?" Craig said. "No way!"

Kenny nodded. "You'll see," he said.

He was right. For the third problem, Ms. Riaz called on Kenny.

Kenny pulled his homework out of his notebook and went up to the board. Ms. Riaz handed him a marker. "Thanks," Kenny said, without thinking about it.

Ms. Riaz looked shocked. "Thank you, Kenny," she replied.

Kenny looked down at his homework. It was a mess, as usual. He started to get frustrated.

I just can't do this stuff, he thought. He was sure the answer on his paper was wrong again.

Kenny wrote the problem on the board. Then he stood back and looked at it.

I can't do this! he thought again. The numbers in front of him started to blur. He couldn't even see straight. He was getting angry.

Then Kenny thought about his last karate class. "It's not the answer you needed, Mr. Parks," Sensei had said. "It is the counting itself." Kenny remembered feeling calmer as he counted.

Kenny closed his eyes and thought about the bus stop. He thought about the people he had counted. He pictured them in his head.

Number 1, the slow old lady. Numbers 2 3, and 4, the high school girls. Number 5, the man with his groceries. Numbers 6 and 7, the mother and her little girl.

As he counted and breathed slowly, Kenny felt himself relaxing. He looked back at the board. The numbers weren't blurry anymore. The question made sense.

Kenny smiled. He lifted the marker and started to write.

* * *

At the end of class, Ms. Riaz asked Kenny to talk to her.

"You did a good job today, Kenny," she said.

"Thanks," Kenny replied. "I can't believe I got that problem right."

"I can," Ms. Riaz said. "I told you that if you could stop letting yourself get frustrated, you'd do great! I'm proud of you."

"Thanks," Kenny said.

Ms. Riaz cleared her throat. "I hope you don't mind me saying this," she added. "Your mother and I were good friends when she taught here. She would be really proud of you."

Kenny swallowed hard and nodded. "I know," he said quietly.

CHAPTER 9

THE BIG DAY

The next few weeks flew by. Whenever Kenny got angry, he would think about the people getting off the bus. He counted them in his head. Every time, his anger faded.

Finally, the day of the tournament had arrived. The morning of the tournament, Kenny's dad drove him to the karate school.

"This is the big day, huh?" Dad asked.

Kenny shrugged, trying to hide his excitement. "Yeah, I guess," he said.

"Good luck," Dad said. "Don't break a leg, okay?"

Kenny laughed as he got out of the car. "I won't," he said.

In class, the students lined up against the wall. "Welcome, students," Sensei said. He smiled.

"As you know, today is the tournament," Sensei went on. "You will all pair up and spar. Each time you strike your opponent, you will earn a point. The winner, after earning three points, will move on in the tournament."

All the students seemed pretty excited. Some were even bouncing on their toes, ready to start.

"In an hour, we will have our class winner," Sensei said. "Count off!"

He paired the students into groups. Then they lined up and faced each other.

"Bow!" Sensei ordered. The class bowed at Sensei, then at each other.

"Begin!" Sensei said.

Kenny took a deep breath. Then he began.

It wasn't like normal sparring. No one spoke or asked who would attack first. They circled each other, looking for ways to strike.

The first four rounds went by quickly. Kenny had practiced so many times with Sensei that the other students couldn't get past his blocks.

Before Kenny knew it, he had made it to the final round. It was between him and Steve Shaw.

They eyed each other and slowly circled. Steve moved forward.

"Hiya!" Steve yelled as he thrust his fist out. Kenny blocked it with ease.

Steve dropped to his knee and swept Kenny's foot. He caught Kenny's ankle and knocked him down.

"One!" Sensei called.

That was a point for Steve. Kenny knew he had to step it up, but he could feel himself starting to get angry.

They started to circle again. Kenny took a deep breath.

He stared into Steve's eyes. "One," Kenny said. "Old lady."

Steve squinted at him. "What?" he asked.

Kenny drew back his elbow. "Two," he said. "High school girl."

He stepped his right foot out and thrust his fist at Steve. "Hiya!" Kenny cried.

Steve blocked the punch. "Dude, what are you talking about?" Steve asked.

Kenny took a deep breath. "Three," he muttered. "Four."

Steve stepped back, then snapped out his leg in a straight kick. "Yah!" he shouted.

Kenny dropped his arms and blocked the kick. "Five," he said. "Big man with groceries."

He pulled on Steve's ankles and dropped his opponent to the mat. "Hiya!" Kenny cried. He dropped his fist onto Steve's chest.

"One!" Sensei called out.

We're tied, Kenny thought.

They began to circle each other again. "Six," Kenny whispered. He took another deep breath.

Steve eyed him and then lunged forward. Kenny brushed the punch aside. Then he landed a kick on Steve's side.

"Two points!" Sensei called out.

Kenny smiled a little. He was winning two points to one.

Steve began to circle him. Kenny could tell Steve was getting frustrated now.

"Hiya!" Steve cried. He quickly threw three punches as he moved toward Kenny. Kenny blocked two of them, but one punch grazed his shoulder.

"Two points!" Sensei called out.

Kenny started to get angry. "What?" he said. Then he stopped himself.

He took a deep breath. "Seven," he said, closing his eyes. "Boy horsing around."

He smiled again and faced Steve. Then he opened his eyes and exhaled slowly.

"Eight," Kenny said, moving forward. "Young mother."

He dropped to his knee and swept Steve's legs. Steve dropped to the mat with a thud.

Kenny quickly stood over him. He drew back his arm. "Nine!" Kenny cried out as he dropped his fist. "Little daughter!"

"Three points!" Sensei called out, stepping onto the mat. "Winner, Mr. Parks!"

Kenny couldn't believe it. Smiling, he got to his feet and offered his hand to Steve.

"Nice match," Kenny said, helping Steve to his feet.

Steve nodded. "You too," he said. "But what was with all that counting?"

Kenny laughed. "It's a long story," he said. "Let's just say all my practice with Sensei paid off."

Kenny looked across the room and smiled at Sensei. Sensei smiled back. Then they both bowed.

ABOUT THE AUTHOR

Eric Stevens lives in St. Paul, Minnesota. He is studying to become a middle-school English teacher. Some of his favorie things include pizza, playing video games, watching cooking shows on TV, riding his bike, and trying new restaurants. Some of his least favorite things include olives and shoveling snow.

ABOUT THE ILLUSTRATOR

When Sean Tiffany was growing up, he lived on a small island off the coast of Maine. Every day, from sixth grade until he graduated from high school, he had to take a boat to get to school. When Sean isn't working on his art, he works on a multimedia project called "OilCan Drive," which combines music and art. He has a pet cactus named Jim.

GLOSSARY

announcement (uh-NOUNSS-muhnt)—something said publicly or officially

energy (EN-ur-jee)—strength

focused (FOH-kuhssd)—if you are focused, you are concentrating on something

frustrated (FRUHSS-trate-id)—feeling helpless or discouraged

level (LEV-uhl)—a position or rank

master (MASS-tur)—expert

ninja (NIN-juh)—a person who is highly trained in ancient Japanese martial arts

opponent (uh-POH-nuhnt)—someone who is against you in a fight

required (ri-KWIRED)—if you are required to do something, you must do it

respect (ri-SPEKT)—a feeling of admiration

tense (TENSS)—nervous or worried

tournament (TUR-nuh-muhnt)—a series of contests in which a number of people try to win a championship

KARATE WORDS YOU SHOULD KNOW

dojo (DOH-joh)—the practice area of a karate school

gi (GEE)—the white robes worn in karate

karateka (kuh-RAH-tee-kah)—a karate student

kata (KAH-tuh)—a pattern of moves used by karate students to practice their skills

kyu (KEE-yoo)—rank, or belt color

sensei (SEN-say)—the teacher of a karate school

spar (SPAHR)—to practice the skills learned in karate classes. Blocks, kicks, and punches are used with little physical contact.

stance (STANSS)—a body's position. There are several stances. Each stance is used for a type of attack or defense.

MORE ABOUT KARATE

Karate is a martial art, or a fighting style. Karate began in Japan. It was first taught in the United States in 1955. Since then, it has become the most common martial art in the United States.

Karate has ranks for levels of skill levels. Each rank has a different belt color. White belts are for beginners. Black belts are for karate masters. It takes years of practice to earn a black belt in karate.

In karate, students learn self-defense. Students are taught many skills, including blocks, stances, punches, and kicks. Students practice by sparring with each other.

Karate involves fighting, but it focuses on self-discipline. Students are taught to respect others and to use fighting as a last resort.

DISCUSSION QUESTIONS

1. Why does Sensei tell Kenny to count the people getting off the bus? How does the counting help Kenny?

2. When Kenny says that the karate school looks gross, Kenny's dad says, "Don't judge a book by its cover." What are some other examples of things that shouldn't be judged by how they look?

3. Kenny uses the counting trick that Sensei taught him to stop feeling frustrated. What are some other ways he could have overcome his frustration?

WRITING PROMPTS

1. Kenny's dad took karate lessons because he, too, had trouble controlling his anger. Pick a person in your family and write about how you are like that person.

2. When he's counting people getting off the bus (on pages 47–49), Kenny sees lots of different people. Choose one of the people he sees. Write a story about what that person is doing that day. Don't forget to give the person a name!

3. Kenny wins the karate tournament. What do you think happens next? Write about it!

INTERNET SITES

Do you want to know more about subjects
related to this book? Or are you interested
in learning about other topics? Then check
out FactHound, a fun, easy way to find
Internet sites.

Our investigative staff has already sniffed
out great sites for you!

Here's how to use FactHound:

1. Visit *www.facthound.com*

2. Select your grade level.

3. To learn more about subjects related
   to this book, type in the book's ISBN
   number: **9781434212009**.

4. Click the **Fetch It** button.

FactHound will fetch the best Internet sites
for you!